THE EXPLODING
SUNS

THE EXPLODING SUNS

Christopher Black

Illustrations by Maelo Cintron

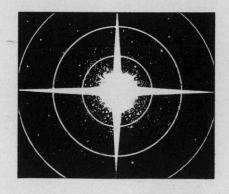

A YEARLING BOOK

Published by
Dell Publishing Co., Inc.
1 Dag Hammarskjold Plaza
New York, New York 10017

Yearling ® TM 913705, Dell Publishing Co., Inc.

ISBN: 0-440-42473-9

Printed in the United States of America

First printing—July 1984

CW

RED ALERT!

You must not read this STAR CHALLENGE AD-VENTURE in the ordinary human way.

If you read the pages in order, the story will not compute. Instead, follow the directions on the bottom of each page. Everything will depend on the choices you make—each choice can lead you to a different STAR CHALLENGE adventure.

To help you along the way, you have a Task/Operational Robot, Model 2. (Call him 2-Tor.) He can do amazing things—from warping you through space faster than the speed of light to talking with you through your mind.

Each time you and 2-Tor complete a mission, warp to page 115 to find out how you rate as a Space Ace!
To begin your adventure, GO TO PAGE 1.

WELCOME ABOARD

The year is 2525 A.D., an age when mankind is moving out among the stars.

You've just come aboard the space station NEBULA, home of the peacemaking and investigation branch of the NETWORK OF WORLDS. From this man-made satellite you, as a NEBULA operative, will go out into the galaxy, taking care of trouble.

The NEBULA's teleportation system can send you anywhere in the galaxy, instantly. Or you can pilot your own shuttle spacecraft, the CHALLENGER. If you need help at any time, feel free to send to the NEBULA for reinforcements.

Remember, the success or failure of your mission (not to mention your own survival) will depend on *your* choices. Successful NEBULA operatives are people who can make quick, thoughtful decisions.

Hurry! CAPTAIN POLARIS needs you!

GO TO PAGE 2.

2

"Come on, boss!" 2-Tor says. You step onto the floating ramp that winds throughout the *Nebula*. The computerized ramp identifies you. Then it moves you into *Nebula* Control. This is the nerve center of all *Nebula* operations. Beings from a thousand worlds monitor a thousand vidscreens. They keep watch for trouble throughout the Network of Worlds.

"I'm glad to see you!" Captain Polaris exclaims. His chair hovers over the controlroom. "There's trouble in Space Sector X-7793A! No time to explain. You have to investigate. Get over to the warping bay. They'll brief you on your assignment."

Captain Polaris taps the keyboard in his chair. Your destination is programmed into the *Nebula* computers. The teleramp rolls you and 2-Tor toward the warping bay.

As you move out of *Nebula* Control, the captain calls, "Good luck! You'll need it!"

Go to the Warping Bay on page 3.

A small creature greets you at the warper room. Eyes rise on stalks from its tiny head. You recognize it as Dr. Zffrr, from the planet Epsilon 12.

"Suns are disappearing in Space Sector X-7793A," Dr. Zffrr says. He hands you a bio-support suit. "You must find out why."

The suit molds itself into a perfect fit around your body. "It will protect you in space," Dr. Zffrr tells you. "It has defensive weapons. A cybernetic relay lets you talk to 2-Tor with your mind. 2-Tor is linked to *Nebula* computers, to access any information you need. He can warp you on command, if you have enough power. That robot is your best friend out there."

Dr. Zffrr asks, "Do you want to warp to Sector X-7793A? Or would you rather fly the shuttlecraft *Challenger*? I'd suggest studying the problem. But I know you action types. Just make up your mind in a hurry. *Nebula* sensors show that another sun just blinked out."

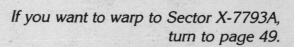

If you want to warp to Sector X-7793A, turn to page 49.

If you want to blast to the stars in the Challenger, *turn to page 44.*

4

You trigger the *Challenger*'s tractor beam. It pulls the Stellar Attack Team's weapons on board. The sunworm wriggles toward another sun.

You study the weapons. "The only thing here that might be useful is a photon cannon," you say. "This could destroy the sunworm. How close would I have to be to use it, 2-Tor?"

The robot's computers whir. "Inside the sunworm, boss," 2-Tor says. "Any other distance has a ninety-nine percent probability of failure."

"We're going in," you tell 2-Tor. You steer the *Challenger* toward the sunworm. The propulsion units are on full. "We'll get that monster before it knows what hit it."

The shuttlecraft shoots into the sun. It rips through the sunworm's glowing skin. Heat beats against you. The ship will melt quickly. How long can you stand it?

If you want to try to get out of the heat, turn to page 63.

If you stay to fire the photon cannon, turn to page 93.

"The warpoon has a megacycle charge in it, boss," 2-Tor says. 'Let's get out of here."

"Right, Tor," you say. "Beam us back to the *Nebula*." Bront comes closer and raises the warpoon. "Hurry up, Tor."

"I can't, boss. We aren't in our own dimension anymore." You stare out the nearest vidscreen. A milky gray blur has replaced the stars. "This ship has shifted into another dimension. I calculate it won't touch our universe again for one hundred years."

The captain stands over you and raises the warpoon. "I'll give you one last chance, mate. Return to your post and I'll forget this ever happened."

You raise your hands to surrender. "Aye, aye, sir," you say. Bront's human lips form a smile. He walks away. He is lost in his madness again.

The hooper leads you to your new cabin. "Look on the bright side," it says. "Life isn't too bad here. And think of the story you'll be able to tell when you get back to the *Nebula*."

"In one hundred years," 2-Tor moans. His lights have stopped flashing. "In one hundred years."

ZAP!

6

Smirking, the alien squeezes the trigger of its weapon. You must think quickly. "Wait!" you shout. "Take me to your commander! I want to join you!"

The Vend laughs cruelly. It pushes you through long corridors. You reach the commander's quarters. They are as cold as space.

For long minutes the alien and its commander talk. At last the commander says, "The warriors of the Vend do not allow aliens into their ranks." You aren't used to being called an alien. On the other hand, this gray lump of a creature has never seen a human before. You are as strange to the Vend as they are to you.

"But . . ." the commander continues. "Tell us about the Network of Worlds' defense system! If you don't— *skrrrk!*" It runs its ragged claw across your throat. Your life depends on your answer.

If you decide to tell the Vend what they want to know, turn to page 48.

If you refuse to talk, turn to page 111.

You leap into the light of the unknown dimension. The starbody gives you a feeling of great power. The energies of the dimension of light pour into you. But you now have too much power. It tears the starbody apart. You dissolve into streams of light, a victim of the unknown dimension.

ZAP!

8

Explosions rock the hive. "Warp us out of here, 2-Tor," you order. "We may not survive in space, but we'll die for sure here." You fade out of the hive.

Suddenly you are floating in space. But your bio-support suit is damaged. "The nearest safe world is seventy-three parsecs away," 2-Tor says. "If we can't recharge, probability of warper failure recharge is ninety-nine percent."

"In other words, we'll never make it," you say. "My suit is ready to fall apart. I don't think I can stay alive in space long enough to recharge." You already have trouble breathing.

"We could send an SOS," 2-Tor suggests. "Probability of that failing is only ninety-eight percent."

If you want to risk warping, turn to page 56.

If you'd rather call for help, turn to page 82.

10

"The team leader has a good idea," you tell 2-Tor. "Vector onto the starship's path." Suddenly you and 2-Tor are dragged into space at warp speeds. The astral winds rip at your bio-support suit, and stars look like blurs as you pass them. The Attack Team is far behind you now.

"What's happening?" you ask.

"Trouble, boss," 2-Tor says. His warning signals flash red. "The starship knows we're following it. It has us in a grabber beam. We'll reach the ship in thirty seconds, whether we want to or not." Sure enough the starship suddenly looms in front of you. "A medium-intensity pulserblast will break us away from their beams."

A bolt of light zips past you. You see that it wasn't aimed at you. Its target is the nearest star. You are still being pulled into the starship.

If you want to go aboard the ship, turn to page 96.

If you choose to follow the lightbolt, turn to page 51.

"We need more help," you say. "Transmit another SOS to the *Nebula*, 2-Tor!"

2-Tor whistles. His blue warning lights blink. "The photon blast ruined my communications equipment, boss. We're on our own."

You rev up the ship's propulsion system. But it just sputters and dies. The explosion has turned the shuttlecraft into a spacewreck. Only the sensors function. They tell you the sunworm is swallowing the *Challenger*. The shuttlecraft begins to vaporize in the heat.

Go to page 63.

The artificial sun moves close. "With luck, I can get one good shot in," you tell 2-Tor. You trigger your micro-pulser.

The blast strikes the center of the sun. Ripples flow across its gaseous skin.

"I've got a new analysis of that thing," 2-Tor bleeps. All his lights are flashing in warning, but his voice is broken by static. "It's not ... warping ... device ..."

"Tor!" you shout. Your voice echoes on your communicator. "What do you mean? What *is* it?"

"Living ..." 2-Tor crackles. "Angry ..."

The warning is too late. Solar flares shoot like fiery arms from the sun-thing. Radiation blinds you, knocking out your sensors.

Then the sun-thing engulfs you. . . .

ZAP!

"To battle stations!" Captain Bront shouts. You, 2-Tor, Bront, and Longhaul race to the ship's vid-deck.

The monitors show a starsnipe swimming through space. The monster is larger than a dozen planets. Captain Bront's starship looks like a speck next to it.

"The starsnipe is heading for an inhabited star system," 2-Tor says. His red lights flash.

"We'll stop it, lad!" Bront cries. "I've waited centuries for this!" He steers the starship after the monster.

"Let me call in a *Network* Defense Team to handle the starsnipe. It will destroy a ship like this."

Bront snarls. His robot hand grips your arm and squeezes. You can't break free. "No," he says. "You might as well kill me now if you do that."

If you do as Bront wishes, turn to page 75.

If you want to call for a Defense Team, turn to page 55.

14

"You are cursed, you who fly on the *Lost Centaurian!*" the cyborg bellows.

"*Cursed? What's he talking about, boss?*" 2-Tor thoughtcasts.

"*Beats me, Tor. And I've never heard of the* Lost Centaurian. *Must be this ship.*"

The cyborg rambles on. "We follow the starsnipe. The foul creature destroyed the homeworlds of every being on this ship. It tore me apart and made me the thing you see." He stares off into space. "Somewhere out there is the great starsnipe. We hunt it! We shall destroy it! Not even death will stop us."

"Excuse me," you say. "Who are you?"

"What?" the cyborg says. It's as if he is seeing you for the first time. "I'm Cap'n Bront, you scurvy dog. Get back to your post! You have to be ready when we face the starsnipe!"

You leave Bront's cabin. "He's a little crazy, isn't he, Tor?"

"He's kweebo for sure," the robot whirs. "What do we do now?"

A creature that looks like a hoop rolls by. "Starsnipe," it says. "All hands on deck!"

"Wait!" you shout. "What's a starsnipe?" The hooper rolls away.

If you want to join the crew, turn to page 65.

If you choose to learn about the starsnipe, turn to page 87.

"The sunworm doesn't answer, Tor," you say. "It must not be intelligent, after all. Signal the squad to attack."

The Stellar Attack Team hurls all its power at the sunworm. Negatron missiles erupt in clouds of light. But the sunworm isn't hurt. Instead, it absorbs the energy. The attack team has run out of weapons.

The monster twists. A rainbow of colors erupts from it, and it looks as if the sunworm is falling into itself. A flash of light as bright as a nova explodes from the sunworm. A new sun forms where the old sun used to be.

Something else appears, too. A face floats among the stars, smiling at you. It is filled with ageless beauty, and it thoughtcasts to you. *"Thank you for keeping me alive. The sunworm was my old form. But I was changing into what you see now. I needed a lot of energy to do it. I'm sorry I was so much trouble, but I'm very far from home. Good-bye, and thank you."* The new creature drifts into space to join the rest of its race in a galaxy far, far away.

---

*You have completed your mission.
Report to the* Nebula *on page 115
to find out how you rate as a Space Ace.*

16

"Lock onto the starship's coordinates, 2-Tor!" you shout. "Let's find out why it's in the area."

"I'm tracking it," the robot replies. "But I'm getting some weird energy feedback ..." 2-Tor's words are cut off. The star with the hole dissolves into fiery splinters. They fade into the cold of space.

"It's horrible," you say. "That star just *collapsed*."

"Boss!" 2-Tor cries. "The starship is changing course. It's heading right at us!"

"Can we avoid collision?" you ask. Your scanners show an open docking bay on the side of the starship, but the bay is closing fast.

"Negative!" 2-Tor's yellow lights flash caution. "The starship is almost on top of us! Eighty-nine percent probability of a crash!"

*If you want to try to get out of the way,
turn to page 99.*

*If you think you can dock in the starship,
turn to page 72.*

You drop to the surface of the planet. Canals crisscross a dense forest of immense, purple flowers. A voice in your mind says, *"Come this way. We need you."*

You wonder where the voice is leading you. You and 2-Tor march through the forest. The forest floor opens. A glowing gas globe rises from the planet's core and surrounds you.

The voice rings in your head again. *"Welcome to our hive. Enter, human, and the secret of the disappearing stars will be yours."*

"Can your sensors find the source of the voice?" you ask 2-Tor. Before the robot can answer, millions of tiny spiral creatures fly out to surround you.

The voice says, *"We are the voice. We have joined our minds together to form one superintelligence called the Hive. Our supermind arranged to bring you here. We have plans for you."* You aren't sure you want to know about their plans.

If you want to try to get away from the Hive, turn to page 29.

If you want to learn more about the Hive, turn to page 104.

18

For long seconds you battle the Stellar Attack Team. "Um, boss ..." 2-Tor says. "These guys don't want to destroy us, but they will if they have to."

"I know," you reply. "But I'm sure the sunworm is intelligent. If it is, *Nebula* regulations won't let us destroy it." But the Stellar Attack Team won't hold off much longer. You reluctantly steer the *Challenger* out of their way.

"Can we communicate with the sunworm?" you ask 2-Tor.

"Possibly," he replies. "But we don't have much time. The sunworm is about to destroy another star."

If you want to try communicating with the sunworm, turn to page 110.

If you decide to let the Attack Team destroy the sunworm, turn to page 95.

"I heard you," you thoughtcast to the supermind. *"You have to keep your side of our bargain."*

"Interesting," says the supermind. *"The starbody has given you greater mental powers. But you are making trouble. We must obliterate you."*

Powerful mindbolts smash you, chipping away at your new body. All your new power can't fight against the supermind for long.

Go to page 83.

20

"*Up shields, Tor,*" you thoughtcast. "*Scan this starship and find out what you can about it.*"

The Vend fires. The blast rebounds off your shield, striking down the Vend warrior. It collapses on the starship deck.

"This hulk is dangerous," 2-Tor gasps. "It's an old-style nuclear vessel with twenty aliens aboard. Odd. They have star-mining equipment. Insufficient data prevents further analysis."

"Nuclear power?" you say. "That hasn't been used since warp drives were invented." Your thoughts are interrupted by the sound of pounding feet. The ship's crew are coming for you.

"Lead the way to engineering, 2-Tor," you say. His red lights flash as he leads you through the starship's corridors. "I've got an idea."

Go to page 41.

"Transmit a message to the *Nebula*, 2-Tor!" you say. "We need help against this monster." The sunworm crawls nearer to the shuttlecraft. There is no reply from the *Nebula*. You switch on the *Challenger*'s propulsion drive, but you can't break free of the stasis web.

A *Nebula* Stellar Attack Team appears nearby. It's armed with high-powered pulser cannons and negatron missiles.

"There's a transmission coming from them," 2-Tor says. "They say they'll handle the situation. They want us to move out of the way."

"We can't!" you say. "We're stuck here!" The Stellar Attack Team has to give up the fight. Or blast through you to get to the sunworm.

If you tell the Attack Team to go ahead despite you, turn to page 47.

If you ask them to wait for you to get to safety, turn to page 85.

You jump into the dimension of darkness. Energy swirls around you, and it eats away at your own power. You're very cold, for just a moment.

Then the energy starts to dissolve *you*. You can't survive in the dark dimension. You begin to glow brighter, until your atoms explode into pure energy. It's the biggest blast ever to happen in this universe. But no one is there to see it. Including you. You have been totally destroyed.

ZAP!

24

The hivebrain slithers toward you. You know it plans to hold you prisoner. "Let's give it a jolt, 2-Tor," you say. A blast from you knocks the hivebrain back. "There's more where that came from. I need answers. Where did you come from and what do you want?"

"One of your scientists created us," the hivebrain reveals. "We steal stars and transmit the energy to our creator. But he enslaves us. We want you to destroy him, so we may be free at last."

"How do I find him?" you ask.

"We'll send you to him, human." A mindbolt strikes you and 2-Tor. The hivebrain says, "Go! Destroy the creator. We have made sure you will not come back to us."

"No! Wait!" you shout. Every cell in your body tingles. Can this being warp you with mindpower alone? There is no time to ask. You and 2-Tor are warping toward an unknown destination.

Go to page 68.

You decide to let the gravity beam take you to its source. Microseconds later you are pulled into a gigantic planet. Like the *Nebula,* everything on this world lives inside it, but a tiny sun lights the planet's core. You've never seen anything like it. When the gravity beam is cut off, you fall up and land.

Crude jewel paws grab you from the glowing rocks you have fallen on. You're in the grip of giant, hulking creatures made of crystal. You hit one, hoping it will break. But the creature is as hard as diamond. "What are these things?" you ask 2-Tor.

2-Tor clicks and whistles. "Insufficient data, boss. Sorry." Their blank expressions tell you the crystal apes are not intelligent. But instead of killing you, they carry you and 2-Tor off.

Go to page 70.

26

"Shut down all power, Tor!" Your mind is clear, even though the sunworm surrounds you. "Manual restart only!"

"But . . ." 2-Tor's blue lights flash.

"Do it!" You can last only ten seconds in space without a bio-support. Ten . . . nine . . . eight . . . The absolute cold of space seeps into you, sapping your strength. Your muscles stiffen. Seven . . . six . . . five . . . You're gambling that you can live longer without life support than the sunworm can live without energy. Your lungs ache from lack of air. Four . . . three . . . two . . . The sunworm spins madly, cut off from its energy source. It is shrinking with every twitch.

Then it's gone. With less than a second to spare you switch bio-support back on. Air fills your lungs.

"Let's not try that again for a long time, boss," 2-Tor says.

"It's a deal," you reply. "Send a message to the *Nebula.* They'd better intercept that starship and stop it from creating more sunworms."

You have completed your mission.
Report to the Nebula *on page 115*
to find out how you rate as a Space Ace.

"Very interesting!" Dr. Leonus says as he studies the cored sun. "A powerful magnetic field holds it open. The magnetic field could distort light and makes it look like the sun disappeared. It makes sense ..."

"I don't want disturb you," you say. "But how does the starship I saw figure in?" As you speak, the starship reappears from warp. It zooms straight into the sun.

"It's an armorstar," 2-Tor says. "One of the most dangerous war vessels in the galaxy. The Vend use them."

"The Vend!" you gasp. "If we're up against *those* warmongers ..."

"It is logical to assume that the Vend are using the cored suns to hide their fleet," Dr. Leonus continues. "We'll have a hard time stopping an entire invasion fleet by ourselves."

*If you want to check out Dr. Leonus's theory,
turn to page 61.*

If you choose to call the Nebula *for reinforcements,
turn to page 39.*

28

"Top speed, 2-Tor!" you shout. Pulserblasts flash around you. The two of you duck into the asteroid belt, narrowly evading the blasts. The force of the pulsers heats the rocky asteroid surfaces to black glass. "Access the *Nebula* and get us some help! Quick!"

But 2-Tor replies, "No good. The starfighters are blocking communications. I can't get data access or warping coordinates."

A nearby asteroid explodes into powder. "We're running out of time!" you shout. "Maybe we should counterattack. They wouldn't be expecting it."

"I wouldn't expect it either," 2-Tor bleeps. "Boss, they outnumber us! Draining your bio-support suit's energies to battle the starfighters could burn it out. You can't risk it."

"2-Tor, we could try to escape, but if that failed . . ."

If you think you should counterattack,
turn to page 34.

If you want to attempt an escape, turn to page 87.

"I'm leaving," you tell the Hive. You switch on your shields. A mindbolt jolts you off your feet.

"We cannot allow you to leave," the Hive says.

"*2-Tor,*" you thoughtcast. *"Compute the frequency the supermind's brainwaves are on, and jam them."* The robot reacts instantly.

You feel the mind fade out of your head. Thousands of the creatures hurl themselves at you and die on your shields.

"Do not think you have won," the Hive says. It speaks now, instead of beaming its thoughts into your head. Then a giant brain crawls toward you. "I am the mind of the Hive," it says. "You will not leave."

If you decide to battle the hivebrain, turn to page 24.

If you want to try to destroy the Hive, turn to page 90.

"We're in trouble!" 2-Tor bleeps.

"Hit them with a wide angle pulser stunburst. Maybe we can scare them off." An arc of light bursts from your pulser and strikes the Saurans.

They laugh. Their body armor absorbed your blast. They keep their distance, but anger rages in their yellow eyes.

"There's a lot of energy under us, boss," 2-Tor says. "We're on a device that collects and stores stellar energy."

"Surrender," you tell the Saurans. They seem to be afraid of the machine. "If you don't, I'll destroy this device!"

An aged Sauran steps forward. "You will destroy yourself as well," it says. "Our stellar collector holds the energy of a thousand suns. That's enough to turn this whole space sector to ashes."

If you choose to destroy the stellar collector, turn to page 45.

If you think you can bluff the Saurans, turn to page 107.

"We have to help them, 2-Tor," you say. "Warp us in." A nanosecond later you are at the edge of an asteroid belt in Space Sector X-7793A.

Starfighters suddenly surround you and fire their pulsers. Your shields ward off the blasts, but only for the moment. "Is there enough power for another warp jump, 2-Tor?" you ask.

"Negative," 2-Tor answers. "Power levels insufficient for 14.3 minutes."

"We can't ward off the pulsers forever. Can we stop all these starfighters by ourselves?"

"Highly improbable," the robot replies. "There is an asteroid belt nearby. Let's take cover there."

"That won't stop the starfighters for long," you say.

If you want to take cover in the asteroids,
turn to page 28.

If you stay to take on the starfighters,
turn to page 89.

32

"I'll keep my side of the bargain," you thoughtcast to the Hive. "If you don't keep your promise, I'll come back to destroy you."

"We agree," the Hive replies. A vidscreen appears on the gaseous wall. "This is a historic event. We are the first beings ever to peek into another dimension."

You look into the scanner. It shows nothing but a patch of darkness and a spot of light. A portal opens on the left side of the scanner, leading to the light. A portal to darkness opens on the right. "You know as much about the other dimensions as we do. Choose one and jump in," the supermind says. "Good luck. Even in the starbody, you may not survive." You look from one portal to the other. Then you make your decision, and jump.

If you choose to land in the darkness, turn to page 23.

If you choose to land in the light, turn to page 7.

You burst out of the storage room and zip toward the captain's cabin. 2-Tor hovers beside you and Longhaul rolls after you.

"What are you going to do?" Longhaul shouts.

"I'm telling Bront the truth!" you say. "I can't believe you've led him on for this long."

You crash through the door of Bront's cabin. "Are you mad?" he cries.

"Listen to me, Cap'n Bront," you say. "There aren't any starsnipes. This hunt is a hoax!"

Bront stares at Longhaul. The hooper cringes. "Explain this," the captain says.

"It's true," Longhaul says. "The crew was helping you to believe in the starsnipe. Hunting it is more fun than what any of us used to do. We're sorry we tricked you."

The starsnipe lurches. Everyone in the cabin is knocked off their feet.

"What was that?" you say.

"I must be going xenkis," 2-Tor bleeps. "My sensors indicate we just got hit by a starsnipe!"

Go to page 13.

34

"We're fighting back!" you say. 2-Tor squeals and hides behind you. The starfighters close in. A jet of light erupts from your autodefense system, striking the nearest starfighter. The hawk-headed pilot writhes and bails out of the damaged ship.

"Come on, 2-Tor," you say. "We're taking over that starfighter! It'll give us the power to fight the others."

Pulsers slice the space around you as you hurl yourself into the abandoned starfighter. But your action was predictable. The others turn on the ship. They blast it—and you—out of existence.

ZAP!

"I'll fight," you tell Commander Kobold. "But your crew surrenders if I win!"

"Agreed." Kobold sneers. "Follow your robot to me—if you dare!" His confidence unnerves you. You follow 2-Tor down the starship's winding corridors. At last you reach the ship's bridge.

From nowhere, the commander jumps you. Kobold's powerdagger barely misses you. He rushes at you again as you switch on your shields. Kobold is twice as big as you and ready to tear you apart.

"*Boss,*" 2-Tor thoughcasts. *"Hit him in the belly as hard as you can."*

You smash him in the waist with both hands. To your surprise, the commander splits in half. Two little aliens crawl out of Kobold. The commander was just a suit, built to scare you with its size. "Don't hit us again," an alien whimpers. "We give up."

"All right, crew," you announce. "Give me information or you'll get the same treatment!" The aliens reveal that they steal stellar energy for an unknown master on a mysterious planet.

"I've recorded the planet's location in my databanks," 2-Tor says.

"Let's go, Tor," you reply.

Go to page 17.

"Our only chance is to capture the lead starfighter, 2-Tor! That might make the others surrender," you say.

"Shields will survive a maximum of twelve mini-pulser blasts," 2-Tor reports. "We may reach the ship before the limit is up." You and 2-Tor zip toward the lead starfighter. Its pulserblasts rock you, knocking you off-course. The eleventh blast rips apart your shields. "We're helpless," you cry.

But you've made it! You crash through the hull of the starfighter. It seals behind you. The captain turns toward you, snarling through blubbery blue lips.

"Surrender!" you say. The alien captain growls. His taloned hand strikes a control panel.

"I die, but you die with me!" it says. You lunge for the ship's controls. The switches glow red hot, and you let go. The last thing you feel is a brief, searing pain as the starfighter blows up.

ZAP!

38

"Tor!" you cry as the sunworm wraps around you. "We have to warp out of here."

"Negative!" 2-Tor replies. "Radiation is disrupting my programming. I cannot link into the *Nebula*'s warping mechanisms until we are clear in space. We're doomed, boss."

Before you can think of another plan, the sunworm squeezes you. Circuits blow out of 2-Tor and your bio-support suit, and the creature absorbs the sparks. You and your 2-Tor heat up. The heat sears you, breaking you into atoms. Then you're energy, a spark between stars. Just a snack gulped up by a hungry sunworm.

ZAP!

"I'm not ready to handle a whole invasion fleet," you admit. "Let's call in a Network task force."

"No!" a voice barks. A Vend warrior has discovered you. Before you can react, it blasts you and Dr. Leonus into unconsciousness. When you wake, you are on a starship. 2-Tor hovers overhead. Dr. Leonus flops beside you, staring blankly.

"Your friend has a powerful intelligence," a Vend tells you. It studies you with the five eyes in its needle-like head. "We have absorbed it into our computers. Your body will be a prize to the leader of the mighty Vend!" With a sneer, the warrior aims his blaster at you.

Go to page 6.

40

You point to the stellar collector, and tell the aged Sauran, "This machine threatens whole star systems."

"Only since the invaders came! Our stellar collector is out of control because of them. It never destroyed stars before! Our other machines are ruined, too. But when we capture the invaders, they die before we can question them."

"Can I see an invader?" you ask.

The Saurans bring a force sphere. "Look at this, 2-Tor," you order, peering at the tiny creatures inside.

"Space bugs!" 2-Tor clicks. "Metal eaters, common to many star systems. They mindlessly eat through machines. But toxins will keep them away. I use such toxins to protect myself."

The old Sauran mutters, "We thought they were an intelligent invasion force."

"We'll get some toxin to you. Then you can fix your stellar collector so that it won't destroy any more stars," you tell the Saurans. "I hope I'll never hear about disappearing suns again."

You have completed your mission.
Report to the Nebula *on page 115*
and find out how you rate as a Space Ace.

"Hold your fire until we reach engineering," you tell 2-Tor. Smashing into engineering section, you shout, "Wide burst, Tor! Now!"

The robot's pulserblast stuns the aliens in engineering. You jam the door closed before the Vend can get in.

"I'm speaking to the leader of the Vend!" you say over ship's intercom. "Tell me why you're destroying stars or I'll blow up this rusty old nuke engine."

The leader transmits back. "This is Garg! We're mining rare gases from the stars. But you'll never tell anyone about it!"

Vend warriors crash in, crying, "Victory or death!"

"Out through the hull!" you tell 2-Tor. Pulserblasts rip around you, and one of them pierces the engines. You and 2-Tor launch into space as the Vend flee for their lives. The ship plunges into the cored star. To your amazement, the star crushes in on the starship. The mining destabilized it, and the end of the ship collapses the star completely. It is the last of the disappearing stars.

*You have completed your mission.
Report to the* Nebula *on page 115
and find out how you rate as a Space Ace.*

42

Io of Shiva grabs at you with its giant, hairy hand.

"Blast it," you tell 2-Tor. A pulserblast from your bio-support suit smashes into Io. It falls back, but it isn't hurt.

Io reaches for a black box made of a metal you've never seen before. "You can't stop me," Io says. "The stolen power of a thousand suns is mine! It's all concentrated in this box. If the *Nebula* doesn't surrender to me, I'll destroy it! Hmmm. You're so small. You must have traveled through my energy collecting system. It compressed you, too. But you know too much!"

"Warp on my command," you thoughtcast to 2-Tor.

"Our power's too low," 2-Tor replies.

"Io has a warper. Trigger it. If Io gets dragged with us, too bad."

"I'll squash you like a bug," Io gloats. It raises its hairy hand to swat you.

Nebula guards blast into the room. Io screams. "What are you doing here?"

"2-Tor accessed the *Nebula*'s intercom when we got here," you say. "Everyone on board heard everything you said, Io."

"I'll still win," Io shouts. It grabs for the energy box. But you and 2-Tor jump for it too. All of you reach it at the same time.

Go to page 43.

"Warp us out as far away from any planet or star as possible, 2-Tor," you shout. You vanish with the box. A micromoment later, you, 2-Tor, and Io are in empty space. Io is startled by the sudden shift. The box falls from its hands. It flies open. The energy inside sweeps over you.

You don't die. Your mind, Io's, and 2-Tor's merge with the energy to form a new supersun. You no longer remember who you were or that you were ever human. As part of a star, you will watch the universe go by forever.

ZAP!

44

"I'll take the *Challenger*, Doc," you tell Dr. Zffrr. You hop onto the ramp that takes you to the shuttlecraft bay. Microseconds later you are in the *Challenger*. The controls hum under your fingers as you glide through hyperspace.

"Why so quiet, 2-Tor?" you say. The *Challenger* has emerged from hyperspace in Sector X-7793A. "This will be an easy mission."

"There is an eighty-seven percent probability of great difficulty," 2-Tor clicks. You laugh. Then you see a star half a light-year away.

The star has a huge hole bored right through the core.

"Unidentified starship is leaving this sector, boss," 2-Tor informs you. "I recommend calling the *Nebula* for mission aid."

If you want to enter the cored star, turn to page 53.

If you decide to investigate the starship, turn to page 16.

If you decide to contact the Nebula *for a backup, turn to page 105.*

The ancient Sauran slithers toward you.

"Get back," you shout. "2-Tor, get ready! Destroy the sun-stealer if the Saurans close in."

"Wait," the Sauran hisses. "We lured you here for the secret of your warper. Give it to us so we can attack the Network of Worlds. Then you can live."

"I don't believe you," you say. "Maybe we can't save ourselves. But we can save the Network of Worlds." You merge your power with 2-Tor's.

"NO!" the Sauran shrieks. "I lied! There's only enough power in the stellar-stealer to destroy this world! Please—don't . . ." But the Sauran is too late. A bolt from your micro-pulser rips through the stellar-stealer. The Saurans scatter, howling in panic. The energy of a thousand suns pours out. You stare in terror as the stellar fury you have unleashed consumes the planet—and takes you and the Saurans with it.

ZAP!

46

"2-Tor!" you think as the spiral creatures dissolve your bio-support suit. "Recircuit my remaining energy to the surface of my suit."

"Your plan has a ninety-nine percent probability of success, boss," 2-Tor says. "Looks good to me." An energy field flares up around you. It shocks the spiraloids. They drop like tiny stones.

"You are too dangerous to live," the Hive thoughtcasts to you. You feel the Hive mind inside your own body, crushing your mind. "Thank you for calling the Nebula," the Hive says. "The Defense Team is already landing outside. Your body will be used to lure them into the Hive. They will be useful in our experiments."

It is the last thing you hear as your mind is destroyed.

ZAP!

"That's it, 2-Tor. Tell the Attack Team to blast through us if they have to," you say.

"Do I have to, boss?" 2-Tor bleeps. But he transmits your message. Nanoseconds later a negatron missile rockets by. You're rocked off your feet as the missile explodes harmlessly against the sunworm. The *Challenger* spins through space, blown free of the stasis web.

A sharp pain jabs your brain. You try to drown out an alien sound. It is the scream of the sunworm. "That sunworm is intelligent," you say. "Or I think it's intelligent. I mean ... I don't know what I mean. It's just a feeling. Maybe we shouldn't let the Attack Team hit it again."

"Illogical, boss," 2-Tor says. "You don't have evidence that it's intelligent, but there's plenty of evidence that it's dangerous. And even if it is intelligent, what if it's an evil intelligence? Can we take that chance?"

"I don't know, Tor," you reply.

If you decide to help the Attack Team fight the sunworm, turn to page 62.

If you think you should save the sunworm, turn to page 114.

48

"Tell us how to smash The *Nebula*," the Vend commander growls. "Now!"

"Access Nebula communications, 2-Tor," you thoughtcast.

"The sun may scramble my transmissions," 2-Tor says.

An urgent message blares from the ship's intercom. "Commander! Our fleet is being fired on—by our fleet!" Sure enough, the monitors show Vend ships fighting each other. "All our crews think the other ships have been taken over by *Nebula* spies."

"You're doing this!" the Vend commander snarls at you. "Stop it!"

"My transmissions fouled up, boss," 2-Tor whirs. *"Sorry."*

"Don't apologize," you say. Then you tell the commander, "Tell your warriors to abandon their ships and get into space. We're going to close up this star. Remember! We can destroy your troops anytime we want to."

It isn't long before *Nebula* squads take the Vend away. You happily watch the stars reappear in the sky.

---

*You have completed your mission.
Report to the* Nebula *on page 115
to find out how you rate as a Space Ace.*

"Warp us to the edge of Space Sector X-7793A, 2-Tor," you say. "I think we should study these vanishing stars before we warp all the way in."

A microsecond passes. You and 2-Tor are no longer in the *Nebula.* You have warped through space. "Let's see a starmap, 2-Tor," you say. The robot's vidscreen lights up with a chart of the area. "There's a pattern. The blanks left by the missing stars form a triangle of circles. It's an interplanetary SOS."

"Someone in Sector X-7793A needs help," 2-Tor says.

"Why would a race so powerful that it can blot out stars need our help?" you ask. "It could be a trap."

If you want to help whoever's sending the SOS, turn to page 31.

If you suspect a trap, turn to page 88.

"Warp us in front of that bolt, 2-Tor," you say. "We haven't got much power left, but warping is the only way to beat the speed of light!"

"Okay, boss," 2-Tor replies. "It means we'll have to abandon the *Challenger*."

"I know," you say, regretfully. When you come out of warp, the lightbolt strikes you. Heat blazes through you. The force swirls around you and begins to take shape.

"It's a sunworm!" you gasp. "Radiate the energy away before it destroys us." But it doesn't work.

"The sunworm's eating our power!" 2-Tor bleeps. "If we don't get rid of it, we'll have seventeen seconds left to live! Get out of range or cut off its energy! Do something!"

If you try to cut off the sunworm's energy, turn to page 26.

If you try warping out of range, turn to page 38.

52

"The sunworm is approaching the *Challenger*. Broadcast my thoughts into space on all frequencies, 2-Tor," you say. Long moments pass, but there is no response. The sunworm draws nearer.

Then space itself begins to shimmer. Two gigantic, radiant creatures appear outside the *Challenger*. They look as if they are made from the dust of stars. Their glow almost blinds you. One of them wraps a shimmering wing around the sunworm.

A voice in your head says, *"Thank you for finding our child."* It is one of the creatures. *"He's just a baby. We're sorry for any damage he caused."*

Before you can answer, all three creatures vanish, streaking off into the unknown. "That's the last we'll see of the sunworm," you say.

"No more suns will disappear now, boss," 2-Tor responds. His yellow lights flash peacefully. "Let's go back to the *Nebula*."

*You have completed your mission.
Report to the* Nebula *on page 115
to find out how you rate as a Space Ace.*

"What's inside that starhole, Tor?" you ask. "Let's blast in." You throw on the *Challenger*'s hyperdrive and soar toward the hole.

But the shuttlecraft suddenly stops. Though its engines hum and strain, it is stuck in space.

"Stasis web, boss." 2-Tor's red warning lights flash. "Someone doesn't want us in that starhole."

"Why not?" you wonder. Your answer crawls out of the starhole. It has thousands of fiery legs and no head. "That thing looks like a giant worm," you mumble.

"No worm ever ate through a sun!" 2-Tor beeps. "We have to get some help. We're sitting quarvers here!"

Go to page 22.

54

The Stellar Attack Team fires negatron missiles at the sunworm. Mighty explosions silently blast the dead of space. But the sunworm is unharmed.

"Wait a minute, 2-Tor!" you say. "The sunworm eats energy. That's why it invades stars, right?"

"Correct, boss," 2-Tor replies. "Why?"

"The attack team threw everything they had at the creature. Now it's bigger than ever."

"Because they fed it more energy," 2-Tor clicks in. "Observation. The sunworm is moving more slowly since the last blast. It may be reaching the limit of energy it can absorb."

"If you're right, Tor ... We should feed it more energy than it can swallow."

Go to page 112.

"Access the *Nebula*, 2-Tor," you say. "Tell them to send a Defense Team after the starsnipe."

Captain Bront lets go of your arm. He sits on the floor and frowns. "Go ahead and kill me. My life is over. All I ever wanted was to hunt down the starsnipe."

"Cap'n! Look!" Longhaul shouts. "The starsnipe is heading back our way. At full speed!"

"It must be attracted by the frequency I'm using to call the *Nebula*," 2-Tor bleeps. "We'll never get out of the starsnipe's way."

Bront leaps to his feet. "Man the blasters! We'll finish the great beastie now!"

But he's too late. The starsnipe's teeth grind down on the starship, crushing everything inside. Captain Bront has met his nightmare, but you have paid the price.

ZAP!

56

"We have to risk warping," you tell 2-Tor.

"Warning! Inadvisable!" says the robot. His red warning lights flash.

"Warp!" The two of you fade.

A terrible pain tears through your body. When it has gone, you feel lightheaded. Then you realize you can see through your hand. "What happened?" you ask 2-Tor. He is transparent, too.

"Warper worked . . . sort of. Part of us reached a planet . . . Part of us remains here . . . systems failing . . . Good-bye . . ."

You wonder if the part of you that warped survived. Then space claims you.

ZAP!

Suddenly the Hive bubbles around you. "Let's get out of here!" you yell to 2-Tor. "It's safer to stay on foot in this chaos." The spiraloids don't seem to notice you. The collective mind that controls them is breaking up, and they are becoming animals again.

You dash down long tunnels until you come to a dead end.

There is only darkness ahead. "Analyze, 2-Tor!" you order. "That may be our only way out of here."

"There is unusual energy," the robot says. "I compute that this is a portal to another dimension. Data is insufficient to determine what lies on the other side." The Hive is disintegrating around you. Through holes in the walls you see the flowered world outside. The whole planet is in flames.

"Attention, boss!" 2-Tor bleeps. "My sensors indicate that if we don't leave the Hive immediately, we'll be destroyed!"

If you decide to jump into the unknown dimension, turn to page 23.

If you risk entering the burning world outside the Hive, turn to page 103.

"That's just legend, 2-Tor. This is ..." You look around. The other beings shuffle around the deck. "What if it's true? What if we can't get off?"

2-Tor stops a woolly-tailed Zu. "Sir! How long have you been on this ship?"

"About three hundred years, small fry." The Zu licks its lips. "I haven't snacked on robots in decades."

2-Tor scurries behind you, out of the Zu's reach. The Zu goes back to its duties.

"Zus usually live about twenty-five years, 2-Tor," you say. "This *is* the *Lost Centaurian*! We have to get off this ship!"

"This is *my* ship!" cries a rasping voice. You turn to see Captain Bront. He carries a warpoon. "*I* say who leaves. Deserters will die!"

If you try to get off the ship, turn to page 5.

If you want to fight with Captain Bront, turn to page 71.

"Shields up, Tor!" you say.

"Watch out, boss!" 2-Tor bleeps. His red warning signals flash with blinding intensity. "Don't you know what will happen when his anti-energy hits our forceshields?" But it's too late.

As the dark light from the negatoid's blaster smashes your shields, explosions rip through the hull of the spaceship. You are sucked through the hole into the vacuum of space.

Your life-support system clicks on. "Look, 2-Tor!" you say. "The explosion has pushed the spaceship into the nearest star."

A dark splotch appears on the surface of the star. 2-Tor's scanners click, and the robot says, "The negatoid is gone, boss."

"Why didn't his anti-energy explode on contact with the star, Tor?"

"It did," he answers. "But he didn't control it this time. The negatoid vanished instead of the star."

"Warp us home, 2-Tor," you say. "I think we've seen the last of the vanishing stars."

*You have completed your mission.
Report to the* Nebula *on page 115
to find out how you rate as a Space Ace.*

60

"Aye!" Bront says. He pulls off his robot hand. Under it is a blaster powerful enough to disintegrate you with one shot. "I must destroy the starsnipe."

"Go ahead," you say. "I'm not going to stop you."

Bront climbs into the nearest ship. It rattles as it takes off. Soon it has vanished against the bulk of the starsnipe.

"I can't believe you let him go," 2-Tor beeps.

"He's got a better plan than I have. Turn on your vidscreen and let's see how he's doing."

You jump out of the way as the rest of the space-ships blast off. Bront appears on 2-Tor's vidcreeen as the spaceships smash into the starsnipe's rocky hide.

"Something's happening to the starsnipe," 2-Tor says. "My sensors show that it's breaking up. Bront is winning." On the vidscreen, you see the starsnipe plunge toward death in a nearby star. Captain Bront rides the monster and laughs wildly. Then both of them are incinerated in the heat of the star.

"Bront finally got what he wanted, 2-Tor," you say. "Our job here is done."

You have completed your mission.
Report to the Nebula *on page 115*
to find out how you rate as a Space Ace.

"We have to investigate the starhole," you tell Dr. Leonus and 2-Tor. As you approach the star, a figure appears in your path. Its head hangs low from massive shoulders. "I am a soldier of the Vend," he says.

Dr. Leonus passes his hand through the soldier. "Curious. It's a light image, a hologram. It can't hurt us." A forcebeam from the hologram blasts you.

"Boss!" 2-Tor bleeps. "Our systems are shut down."

Dr. Leonus salutes the hologram figure. "I'll return to the *Nebula* now and continue to spy on the Network of Worlds. Hail the Vend." He vanishes. Then you and 2-Tor blink out, too.

You're warped aboard an armorstar, hidden in the starhole. *"That blast wasn't too bad,"* 2-Tor thoughtcasts. *"Our systems are working again."*

Another Vend grabs you. "Welcome, spy!" it growls. "The sentence for spying is death."

If you think you can outwit the Vend, turn to page 6.

If you try to defend yourself, turn to page 20.

62

"The attack team won't be able to reload before the sunworm gets them," 2-Tor says.

"Thanks to them, the *Challenger* is free of the stasis web," you say. You blast in to help the team. But the sunworm has gotten there well before you. Before your eyes the attack team is vaporized in the worm's heat. A few weapons survive, floating in space.

"We need more help, boss." 2-Tor's blue lights flash. But you are eyeing the weapons.

If you decide to use the Attack Team's weapons, turn to page 4.

If you'd rather send for more help, turn to page 11.

"Blast off, 2-Tor," you say. "We're getting out of here." The meganium walls of the *Challenger* turn to liquid. The heat is unbearable, but it only lasts for a moment. You rapidly cool off.

"Report, 2-Tor! Where are we?"

You seem to be on land, but the "ground" is warm—and alive. The sky shimmers with a rainbow of radioactive colors.

Before your robot friend can respond, you hear a hollow voice. "Forgive me. I did not speak your language. I thought you were two of the space parasites that sometimes live on my skin. Only when you were about to die did I realize you were intelligent beings."

"By the asteroids of Katar!" you exclaim. "2-Tor! We're inside the sunworm!"

"I brought you to the one part of me where you won't be hurt," the sunworm says. "It was the only way for you to survive."

"Thanks," you answer. "Can you drop us off at the *Nebula*?"

"No," the sunworm says. "If you pass through me, you'll be destroyed. You'll have to live inside me forever. I'm sorry."

ZAP!

"*Quick, 2-Tor,*" you thoughtcast. "*Send a homing transmission to the* Nebula. *They'll track us to this planet. Tell them to warp in a defense squad with mindshields.*"

"*You are not worthy to take part in our experiments,*" the Hive says. "*We will destroy you, and set another trap for the people you have called.*"

Spiraloids swarm from the gaseous walls of the Hive. Thousands crawl over you until you are covered with them. The spiraloids gnaw through the circuits of your bio-support suit.

2-Tor's flashers go from blue to red. "Damage to bio-support is approaching unacceptable levels. If we don't get away soon, you'll be doomed." But if you don't stay, the *Nebula* Defense Team will warp into a Hive trap.

If you think you can hold off the spiraloids, turn to page 46.

If you choose to get out while you can, turn to page 86.

The hooper rolls away before you can catch up to him. "This ship is screwy," you tell 2-Tor. "Let's join the crew and find out what's going on."

You reach the deck. The crewmembers are aliens from a hundred different planets. You see spiked Entens from the colonies of Karsh, and split-eyed Ummas from Lagash.

"How did Captain Bront get so many different beings together?" you say. "Oh, oh. I think I've heard of the *Lost Centaurian* before. But where?"

2-Tor's circuits snap. "It's a legend, boss. The creatures of Dahma scare their kids with it. The *Lost Centaurian* is a ghost ship that sails the stars forever. If it catches you, you'll never get off it."

Go to page 58.

"There are too many starfighters, 2-Tor," you say. "If we can get away from here, we can contact the *Nebula* for help." But starfighters already swarm around you. Your blood curdles when you see the grinning, hawk-beaked faces of your enemies.

"Incoming message," 2-Tor beeps. "It's one of the starfighter pilots."

"You can't escape," the pilot says. "When will we move in for the kill? When will we tire of toying with you?" It laughs.

The laughter is cut off as a lightblast rips through the starfighter formation. "Someone's helping us, 2-Tor," you say. The communications from the starfighters have stopped. "We're saved!"

"Um, boss ..." Tor replies. His blue lights flash a warning. "I don't think we're out of trouble yet."

A fleet of starcruisers from deep space are rounding up the disabled starfighters. "I don't know if they're friend or foe," you say. "But I think we're going to find out."

Go to page 81.

68

Your head buzzes. "We're on some sort of spaceship, 2-Tor," you say. But everything around you is a thousand times bigger than normal. 2-Tor hums back to life next to you.

"Sensors indicate that this is the *Nebula*," 2-Tor bleeps.

"What happened?" you ask. "How did the ship get so large?"

"It didn't," the robot answers. "We became tiny. Approximately the size of a Neptunian moonfly. Our circuitry is supercharged, too."

"Supercharged?" You stop speaking. A hairy humanoid with wide pointed ears enters the chamber. "That's Io, the ambassador from the planet Shiva. What's he up to?"

Io speaks to a robot that hovers next to him. "How much stellar energy has been transmitted to me?" it asks.

But the robot replies, *"Alert! Alert! Unauthorized intruders!"* Shocked, Io looks around and sees you. With a sneer, it reaches for you.

If you try to warn Captain Polaris about the traitor, turn to page 74.

If you try to stop Io, turn to page 42.

"2-Tor!" you say. "Those Saurans' scales are natural. It's not wargear. They may not be hostile, after all."

You raise your arms and press your fingers together over your head. You have made the interplanetary peace sign. The Saurans seem to relax.

An ancient Sauran with deep cracks in its hide steps forward. It speaks in a language you don't understand.

"No sweat, boss," 2-Tor clicks. "I can translate."

Nanoseconds later you hear the old Sauran say, "We need your aid. Enemies have invaded our world. They are using our machines for evil. We were afraid you might be one of them, but you don't look like the creatures we captured."

"Look," 2-Tor says. An image appears on his vidscreen. It is a stellar collector. Moments later you see the stellar collector among the Saurans' machines.

Go to page 40.

70

The crystal apes glint in the green light at the world's core. They drag you to a platform carved from stone.

They drop you and 2-Tor there, then dance around the platform. Their crystal bodies chime as they dance. The sun inside the planet pulses in rhythm with their chiming. "Scan that sun, 2-Tor," you say.

"I'm way ahead of you, boss," the robot bleeps. "That's no sun at all. It's a matter-teleportation unit. Like a warper."

"Then why is it grabbing us?" you ask. A gravity beam clutches you. But you and 2-Tor rise toward the sun.

"My bio-support suit won't respond, Tor! Can you warp us out of here?"

But 2-Tor's reply is broken by static. "I am experiencing electromagnetic interference ... warper inactive ... difficult to communica ..."

"2-Tor? 2-Tor! We've got to do *something!*"

·If you decide to fire your pulser at the sun, turn to page 12.

If you decide to wait and see what's going on, turn to page 68.

"I'm a trained *Nebula* operative," you say. "You'll get hurt if we fight."

Captain Bront slashes at you with the warpoon. "I've fought tougher beings than you and lived to talk about it!" You back away from the deadly blade.

"2-Tor!" you shout. "Plan Z-211." A cable snakes from the robot's chest. Sparks fly as it touches the captain's metal skin. You box Bront's human ear at the same time. Stunned, Captain Bront falls to the deck and blacks out.

"Let's get out of here," you say.

"Something's wrong, boss," 2-Tor bleeps. His red lights flash. Then you notice you can see through your hand. The rest of the crew is becoming transparent, too.

"You fool!" the hooper shouts. "Don't you know what you've done? This whole ship was Captain Bront's fantasy. We were here because he believed in us. Now that he's unconscious, we'll cease to exist—"

The hooper never finishes. But that's all right, because you aren't there to hear him.

ZAP!

72

"Hang on, 2-Tor," you cry, and you trigger the *Challenger*'s hyperdrive. You roar at the starship.

"Please don't do this, boss," 2-Tor beeps. His red lights flash. "A shuttlecraft attack on a starship has a one hundred percent probability of failure."

"I'm not attacking, Tor. I'm docking!"

"At *this* speed? The docking bay opening on the starship is too narrow! The *Challenger* will *never* pass through," he says. "We'll crash."

"Care to bet?" you ask. 2-Tor covers his vidsensors. You rotate the *Challenger.* Seconds before you'll crash, you fly the shuttlecraft into the docking bay sideways. Screaming aliens leap out of the way. Just before you smash against the back wall, you spin the shuttlecraft around. The *Challenger* skids into the wall, but you are unhurt.

You and 2-Tor stagger out of the shuttlecraft. Ball-shaped aliens, three feet tall, rush toward you. Before they can reach you, a thin, cruel face appears on a vidscreen in the docking bay. Three eyes, one above the other, stare from the face.

Go to page 73.

"Let no one touch this *Nebula* operative!" the alien commands. Its crew backs away from you. "I am Kobold, commander of this vessel, human! In honor of your bravery, I offer you an opportunity. You may die in hand-to-hand combat with me."

"And if I don't like that idea?" you ask.

"Then my crew will take your life-support systems and you will be thrown into space." The crew presses eagerly toward you.

If you accept the alien's challenge, turn to page 36.

If you want to take your chances against the crew, turn to page 101.

Io's outstretched hand is closing around you. You shout, "2-Tor! We have to warn the captain! Propulsion! Now!" Both of you dart away from Io's grip. The alien chases you around the chamber, but he can't grab you.

"You blundering fool!" You and Io turn to face a hulking, four-armed alien—Hosh, the *Nebula*'s chief engineer.

"No! It wasn't my fault," Io whimpers. Hosh silences it with a blast from her micro-pulser.

"It's so hard to get decent help these days," Hosh says. She stares at you. Then she picks up a metal plate in each hand. "I see you've been caught in one of my energy concentrators. The effects aren't permanent. You'd be full size in an hour."

She hefts all four plates over her head. "But you'll be flatter than a bug by then."

Go to page 78.

"All right, captain," you say. "I'll give you one chance. Then I'm calling in a Defense Team."

Bront's robot eyes gleam. "Full speed ahead," he shouts. "I know more about the starsnipe than any other being in the galaxy."

He stomps to a docking bay filled with old spaceships. Some of them haven't been used for hundreds of years. "You aren't going to use *these,* are you?" you ask.

Bront grins. "A starsnipe lives in space. There isn't sound or air in space. So sound and air will kill a starsnipe. These ships will attack it with sound and air."

"There are a lot of ships," you say. "Who will fly them to the starsnipe?"

"They'll be led there," Captain Bront says. He pulls a small homing beacon from his pocket. "With this."

"Boss!" 2-Tor beeps. "Bront wants to put that beacon on the starsnipe *himself!*"

If you let Bront carry out his plan, turn to page 60.

If you want to attack the starsnipe yourself,
turn to page 109.

"Someone wants to capture us, 2-Tor," you say. "Can you trace that gravity beam?"

"Sure thing, boss," 2-Tor replies. "I've got a fix on it already. What should we do?"

"Let's give them a surprise. Add our power to the beam. We'll get to our kidnappers sooner than expected. It might give us an edge."

You land on a desert planet. Scaled, lizardlike aliens, bigger than you, are gathered around a humming device. It projects a hot light toward the stars. The lizards' hides are protected by armor that looks like it's made from protanium.

"Identification," 2-Tor says. "The lizards are similar to the Saurans of the Dojan system."

You realize that light isn't going to the stars. It's coming *from* the stars.

"2-Tor," you whisper. "That's what they're using to steal starpower." You and 2-Tor land next to the stellar collector. The Saurans stare at you warily. They're preparing to attack.

*If you want to scare off the Saurans,
turn to page 30.*

If you'd rather make peace, turn to page 69.

"The spy is a greater threat than the starfighters," you say. "Are your controls still blocked, Tor? Can you warp us back to the *Nebula?*"

"They dropped the interference to make the sub-space call," 2-Tor clicks. "We can warp anywhere."

A familiar light surrounds you. In a nanosecond you're back in the *Nebula's* energy room. All the ship's power comes from here.

"Hey! You're not permitted in this area!" shouts the chief engineer. She's a four-armed Jovian named Hosh. Her dark eyes glow with an angry light.

"*Nebula* business. I'm tracking a spy," you tell her. "We traced secret communications to this place."

"No one's here but me," Hosh says. "There must be an error."

2-Tor's blue lights flash. "I'm *not* wrong. Hosh has an unauthorized communicator on her belt."

Hosh throws herself at you, swinging her four powerful arms. You back away from her. "Captain Polaris will want to hear about this," you say.

"You won't live to expose me." She growls.

Go to page 78.

Hosh gloats. "My agents are stealing energy from the stars. Soon we'll have enough to take over the Network of Worlds! My starfighters will draw off the *Nebula* fleet. And I'll destroy the *Nebula*."

Before she can strike, you discharge all your energy through your micro-pulser at her. Hosh topples. Her dreams of conquest fall with her.

"You could have blasted her all along, boss," 2-Tor whistles. "Why did you act helpless?"

"I wanted to get a confession, Tor." You tap your suit's built-in recorder. "It was the only real proof I could get against Hosh. Now we can undo her plotting. She'll go to a prison asteroid for good."

You have completed your mission.
Report to the Nebula *on page 115*
to find out how you rate as a Space Ace.

You enter the corridor. A crackling voice says, "What have you there, mate? Is it mutiny you're plotting?"

"Oh, no!" 2-Tor clicks. "We're grist now!"

"Quiet, 2-Tor," you thoughtcast. You hand the helmet to Captain Bront. "Forgive us for not being at our posts, sir. We were making this helmet. It'll help you find the starsnipe."

"Aye?" The Captain grabs the helmet and puts it on.

"Now, Tor!" you cry. A spark flies from 2-Tor and strikes the helmet. Captain Bront freezes where he stands.

"What have you done to him?" Longhaul the hooper says. "Curse the day you set foot on this ship."

"We've solved everyone's problems," you say. "The helmet is linked into Bront's robot eye now. It will always show him pictures of the starsnipe. The hunt will go on forever, but only in his mind. The crew can go home now, Longhaul. You don't have to destroy any more stars."

You have completed your mission.
Report to the Nebula *on page 115*
to find out how you rate as a Space Ace.

80

"The team leader is right," you say. "We won't survive a direct assault on the sunworm. We have to think of something else."

Before you can act, the sunworm bursts from the starhole. The star collapses into itself, re-forming into a smaller, brighter star.

"My sensors are tracing the sunworm," 2-Tor says. "It's stopping in the middle of nowhere, boss. I was sure it would head for another star."

"Let's follow it," you say. You steer the *Challenger* through the depths of space. When you reach the sunworm, it spins. It begins to change. "What's happening to it, Tor?"

"It . . ." Even 2-Tor is stunned. Then you see your answer. This is the final fate of the sunworm—it has become a beautiful, glowing gas ball.

"How about *that*?" 2-Tor beeps. "I always *wondered* where baby stars come from."

You have completed your mission.
Report to the Nebula *on page 115*
to find out how you rate as a Space Ace.

One of the starcruisers hovers next to you and 2-Tor. An airlock opens. "Should we go in?" 2-Tor asks.

"I can't think of a better way to find out what's going on, Tor. But keep your defenses up, just in case." You enter the starcruiser warily.

You are met by a black feathered alien. "I sense you are puzzled," it says. "Fear not! We are friendly. My name is Greep Dunzag."

"Was your race responsible for the vanishing stars, or did the hawkheads cause that?" you ask, fingering your micro-pulser.

Greep Dunzag laughs. "My people warped the starlight. It only looks as if the stars are gone. The hawk-headed aliens had threatened to destroy us. We hoped a fleet would come to our aid.

"When you arrived alone, we thought all was lost. But then the hawkheads attacked you, and it gave us the chance to counterattack them. Thank you for your help." The stars begin to reappear. 2-Tor's yellow lights glow.

You have completed your mission.
Report to the Nebula *on page 115*
to find out how you rate as a Space Ace.

"We shouldn't warp now," you tell 2-Tor. "Do we have energy to send a subspace communication?"

"Sure, boss," 2-Tor replies. "But the energy loss will make survival improbable."

"Survival is already impossible, 2-Tor," you reply. "We have to take any chance we have."

2-Tor broadcasts a subspace message until his power dies. Your bio-support suit also runs out of power. The cold of space begins to grip you.

Then it is warm. You and 2-Tor have been warped aboard the *Nebula*.

Captain Polaris enters through the warp bay door. "We thought we lost you," he says. "Have you learned why the stars were disappearing?"

"It's a long story, sir," you say. "Almost too hard to believe. At least we won't have to worry about vanishing stars anymore."

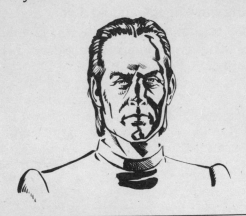

You have completed your mission.
Report to the Nebula *on page 115*
to find out how you rate as a Space Ace.

"I'll show you what power I have," you thoughtcast to the Hive. You concentrate. *"There are a thousand stars in this body. If they're forced together tightly enough, they will either explode or form a black hole."*

The Hive screams as it realizes it has made a fatal mistake. You use the starbody's energy to levitate 2-Tor and your body into space.

"We'll destroy you before you destroy us," the Hive says. You feel the crush of its mighty intelligence. It is too strong for you. Psychic energies swirl around your collapsing starbody. The pressure is more than you can stand.

You hurl your mind from the starbody toward your real body in space. Below you the planet collapses. A black hole forms from the starbody, and draws the planet into it. Then you are alone with 2-Tor. The planet, the starbody, and the Hive are all gone. There won't be any more disappearing stars.

You have completed your mission.
Report to the Nebula *on page 115*
to find out how you rate as a Space Ace.

84

"We're going to blast this Hive into hyperspace, 2-Tor," you say. "Unleash micro-pulsers at full force." The gas wall of the Hive bursts into flame from the heat of your blast. Your vision has become reality.

"Ha," the Hive says. "That won't stop us!" A supermindbolt smashes you through the wall. "You see, human. We shall finish you off now."

"Prediction," 2-Tor says. "The Hive can either destroy us or save itself. It doesn't have time to do both."

"You're lying!" the Hive snarls. But the whole place has ignited. The Hive has wasted its last seconds. Then it screams, and darkness overwhelms you.

You wake up several hours later. 2-Tor hovers protectively above you. "All that's left of the Hive is a few burning gasballs, boss," 2-Tor says. In the sky above, you see the stars—stars that will never vanish, thanks to you.

You have completed your mission.
Report to the Nebula *on page 115*
to find out how you rate as a Space Ace.

You transmit to the Stellar Attack Team. "Give me time to break out of this stasis web." You tell 2-Tor, "Quick! Recircuit the *Challenger*'s engines to absorb the web energy! We have only seconds!"

"Incoming energy is overloading us, boss," 2-Tor bleeps. "We'll melt if we don't get rid of it soon."

"Hang in there for a little longer, 2-Tor." Your sensors reveal that the web is breaking down. But the *Challenger*'s walls are glowing. "Hit thrusters! Now!" The *Challenger* lurches and breaks loose from the web.

You contact the Attack Team again. "What can I do to help?"

"Follow the starship that left this thing!" the team leader orders. "Leave the sunworm to us."

*If you choose to help the Attack Team,
turn to page 54.*

If you agree to follow the starship, turn to page 10.

86

"We're getting out of here," you tell 2-Tor. "Propel us off-planet!" You soar through the gaseous wall. But then you freeze in the air, unable to rise.

"Fool!" the Hive says. *"You will not leave, no matter how much you struggle."*

"It gets worse, boss," 2-Tor whistles. "The Network operatives you called are warping in. If we don't do something in seconds, they'll be trapped like us!"

"There's one chance, 2-Tor. Can we change the gas the Hive is made from?"

"Affirmative," 2-Tor replies. "An electromagnetic discharge will break down the walls."

Switching your pulser to electrical output, you blast the Hive. A dazzling light glows around it. The Hive evaporates. As your backup from the *Nebula* warps onto the planet, the spiraloids wriggle on the ground, gasping.

"You cut off their air," 2-Tor reveals. "It's the end of the Hive."

You have completed your mission.
Report to the Nebula *on page 115*
to find out how you rate as a Space Ace.

The hooper stops. "I don't believe I've seen you on board before, mate," it says. "You're the lads we pulled off the hull?"

"Right," you say. "You shot down our shuttlecraft."

"Oops. Sorry about that," the hooper says. "We were practicing for a starsnipe hunt. By the way, I'm Longhaul. You couldn't pronounce my real name."

"Starsnipe!" 2-Tor says. "A fantastic beast said to roam space, gulping down suns and worlds. It's a fairy tale. Why do you hunt a fairy tale?"

"Hush, mate. Come with me." You and 2-Tor follow it down a dozen corridors. At long last you reach a small room filled with supplies.

"We can speak freely here, mate. Of course there are no starsnipe. But the cap'n thinks there are, and we'll follow him anywhere. If we told him the truth, he wouldn't have anything to live for. We wipe out a star once in a while to give him something to hunt."

"You can't do that," you say. "It's crazy."

"I can't let you stop us," Longhaul says. "It'll kill the cap'n!"

If you think it best to tell Captain Bront the truth, turn to page 33.

If you want to try saving Captain Bront, turn to page 102.

88

"I think we're being led into a trap, Tor," you say. "Abandon the mission. We need heavily armed help."

A high-intensity lightray appears from the depths of space. It sweeps over you and 2-Tor. "We're in the grip of a gravity beam!" you shout.

"I'd find out where we were going, boss," 2-Tor clicks. His blue lights flash. "But I'm afraid to ask."

If you choose to ride the beam, turn to page 25.

If you decide to rush ahead of the beam, turn to page 76.

"Can you scan the enemy's computers?" you ask 2-Tor.

"Affirmative, boss! I'm computing the starfighters' targets. Patch that data into your bio-support suit's computer, and you'll easily avoid their blasts."

You zip between two ships. Their computers track you. The two ships blast each other. The others are afraid to attack you now, afraid the same thing will happen to them.

"I'm monitoring a subspace communication," 2-Tor says. "The lead starfighter is contacting the *Nebula*! They're calling for *help!*"

You are shocked. "Our people wouldn't help them against us! The starfighters must have a spy on the *Nebula* itself!"

If you decide to track down the spy, turn to page 77.

If you want to continue the battle, turn to page 37.

90

You thoughtbeam to the Hive, *"If you don't free us, 2-Tor and I will destroy the Hive."*

"We could destroy you in a nanosecond, foolish human," the Hive says. *"Your pitiful defenses can't stop us."*

A powerful mindbolt smashes through your shields. Energy crackles from the broken circuits of your bio-support suit.

"Damage report, 2-Tor?" It feels like your brain is shorting out, too.

"We're out of control," the robot replies. "Warping and bio-support functions took a direct hit. But the Hive is out of control, too. It discharged more energy than it could stand."

It's true. All around you spiraloids wither and disintegrate. The hivewalls shake and crack. In the middle of it all, psionic sparks fly from the Hive. The part of it that is closest to being a face twists in pain.

"Let's get out of here, 2-Tor," you say. "Anything is better than staying in this deathtrap!"

If you want to risk warping away, turn to page 8.

If you want to run away on foot, turn to page 57.

Before the Attack Team can open fire, a gigantic alien spaceship appears. "Why have you invaded our project?" booms a voice that can be heard even through the vacuum of space.

"We chose this sector because it was uninhabited. There is no danger. Our creation has absorbed enough energy for its final transformation. Look, beings from the Network of Worlds, and see wonder in the making!"

You stare in amazement as the sunworm returns to the starhole. In a blinding flash of light the worm and the sun become a single solar ball. It explodes across the sky like a living rainbow. Space itself swirls around the creature. The sunworm leaps from the solar ball and shoots off into the galaxy.

"Beautiful, boss," 2-Tor says. "We just saw the birth of a living comet."

"I wonder how those aliens in the spaceship did it," you say. You look around. The spaceship has vanished. The aliens and the sunworm are gone, taking their mysteries with them.

*You have completed your mission.
Report to the* Nebula *on page 115
to find out how you rate as a Space Ace.*

92

"Hold your fire!" You frantically transmit to the Stellar Attack Team. "I suspect the sunworm is intelligent. I want a chance to communicate with it!"

"If we take any time, no one will have a chance," the team leader replies. "That monster is a threat to the whole galaxy! Now, get out of our way. If you don't, we'll have to destroy you with the sunworm!"

Go to page 91.

The heat inside the monster is unbearable. But before the sunworm can vaporize you, you trigger the pulser cannons. As the weapons are about to explode, you shout, "2-Tor! Channel all energy to our shields!"

"Boss! That won't protect us against all this pow—" Forcewaves smash against you and 2-Tor as the cannons blow. You black out.

When you wake up the only light you see is from the last wisps of the sunworm. You have destroyed it, but at a terrible price. Bits and pieces of 2-Tor float around you. He must have sent all his energy into your shield instead of his own.

"You gave your existence for me, 2-Tor. I'll never forget you."

"Gee, I hope not, boss," says your little friend's voice. Then you see a glowing yellow memory chip linked to a communications module. 2-Tor is still there, if not in one piece. "I'm accessing the *Nebula* now. When we get back, have them put me in a new body, OK?"

"You bet!" you cry. "Dr. Zffrr was right. You're the best friend I have out here, Tor!"

You have completed your mission.
Report to the Nebula *on page 115*
to find out how you rate as a Space Ace.

"2-Tor?" you ask. "Can you scan the sunworm for brainwaves? The creature could be intelligent."

"Negative, boss," 2-Tor says. "You've been had. The sunworm doesn't have brainwaves. It doesn't even have a brain!"

"But . . . we both heard it!"

"Negative. I compute that we heard *your* brainwaves, fed back at us. It's the sunworm's natural defense mechanism."

"It's a trick!" you shout, as you access the *Nebula* Attack Squad. "Blast that monster out of the sky!"

The squad bombards the star with negatron missiles and anti-matter charges. The sun erupts, and collapses into a black hole.

The sunworm squirms, but it is caught by the black hole's awesome gravity. It disappears forever into the last of the vanishing suns.

You have completed your mission.
Report to the Nebula *on page 115*
to find out how you rate as a Space Ace.

96

"We're boarding that spaceship," you tell 2-Tor. The two of you rocket toward it. No one aboard seems to pay attention as you climb through an airlock into the ship. Once on the ship's bridge, you are puzzled by the crew.

"They're humanoids, Tor. But . . . it's as if they were photographic negatives." You brush your fingers warily on a crewmember.

You're thrown across the room. A nanosecond later shockwaves and a loud roar hit you.

"Observation, boss," 2-Tor says. His blue lights caution you. "These beings are made of negative energy. Contact with your positive energy could result in disaster."

"Listen to the robot," a threatening voice says. "Your suit saved your life, but my brother didn't have that kind of luck! He's dead—because you touched him!"

You wipe the smoke from your eyes and stare at the being who stands over you. "Wh-what are you?"

Go to page 97.

"Negatoids. We come from a negative universe," the being says. "We need energy for our galaxy. The sunworm devours stars. Then it changes their energy from positive to negative, and transfers the energy to our universe. We can't permit you to interfere."

"That's monstrous," you shout. "If you take all our stars, our galaxy will die."

The negatoid shrugs. "Your universe is unimportant. When your worlds are gone we'll take over here, too. But you'll die long before your galaxy ..." A blaster materializes in the Negatoid's hand. "Good-bye."

Go to page 59.

98

"Dying doesn't exactly thrill me," you say. You trigger the *Challenger*'s thrusters. "But there's no time to think of a better plan." The shuttle blasts into the sunworm's great maw. Its shields begin to buckle under the tremendous heat in the creature's belly. The *Challenger*'s control panel is too hot to touch.

"Get ready to warp us out of here, 2-Tor," you say. "I'm going to trigger the shuttle's self-destruct circuit."

"We shouldn't warp, boss," 2-Tor beeps. "Too much stellar radiation around. I can't compute a warp-out point. We could reappear anywhere—a planet's crust or right back here."

"There's no time to plan, 2-Tor! Warp!" Your hand slaps the self-destruct button. You're no longer there.

You rematerialize in space, millions of miles away. In the distance the sunworm shifts from color to color. It explodes, spewing gas and radiation throughout the sector. From where you hover, it looks like a beautiful exploding sun.

You have completed your mission.
Report to the Nebula *on page 115*
to find out how you rate as a Space Ace.

You slam on the *Challenger*'s thrusters and rocket out of the starship's path. A puff of light, like a tiny comet, rushes at you from the starship.

"Negatron torpedo, boss," 2-Tor bleeps. "Our shields can't stand up to it. There's not a chance in Nyx we can outrun it. Abandon ship?"

"You said it, 2-Tor." Both of you leap through the emergency airlock.

The *Challenger* vanishes in a soft puff of black light. Shock waves press you against the hull of the starship. You are still there moments later when crewmembers arrive to pull you from the hull.

"Do we attack, boss?" 2-Tor whistles.

"We'll find out what's going on a lot easier if we get ourselves captured, Tor. Put up shields only if they try to hurt us." The crew hauls you into the starship.

Soon you face the starship's captain. Half his body is human, but the other half is a machine covered with plastic skin. He glares at you with a computerized eye.

"He's a cyborg," 2-Tor thoughtcasts to you.

"Shhh!" you say. *"He's going to speak!"*

Go to page 14.

100

"How about making a deal?" you ask.

The Hive laughs. "We do not make deals with inferior beings."

You try to move, but the Hive has stolen control of your body. A single spiraloid rises to your forehead. It unwinds to form a living link between you and the starbody. You feel your mind sliding down the spiraloid. In that moment you are one with the spiraloids and the supermind.

You imagine a horrible disaster. The Hive explodes in flames like a small nova star, scorching and slaughtering millions of spiraloids.

The vision is too much for the Hive. In panic, it lets you go, to slide back into your body. It may have been the stronger intellect, but you have the more powerful imagination.

"You must not go free," the Hive snarls as it regains control. "If you will not serve us, you must die."

If you want to try to destroy the Hive, turn to page 84.

If you decide to call for help, turn to page 64.

"We can't trust Kobold," you tell 2-Tor. "Where's his transmission coming from?"

"My sensors read that he is three decks up," 2-Tor replies. "I compute that he is setting a trap for us."

"Only a Vegan wobat would walk in Kobold's front door, 2-Tor. It'll sap our power, but I want to cut through these walls and sneak up on him."

Your micro-pulsers melt the ship's wall to slag. You picture the look that will be on the commander's face when you burst in on him. "Deck Three coming up," 2-Tor beeps. "Get ready, boss!"

The wall melts away. You leap onto the bridge. A dozen armed aliens surround you. All are ready to pulser you into oblivion.

"We were expecting your little trick," Commander Kobold says with a smirk. "Farewell, *Nebula* operative."

Go to page 106.

102

"There's a way to give Bront his hunt and end it at the same time," you say. "Do you have any spare robot parts around here?"

Longhaul blinks. "Aye, but . . ."

"Show us the way," you say. Moments later Longhaul leads you into an old workshop. It hasn't been used in years. Computer chips and bits of machinery litter the floor.

"Access the *Nebula,* 2-Tor. We need plans for vidscreens and hologram projectors." The robot clicks and whirs.

"Got it, boss," 2-Tor says. "Let's get started."

For long hours you and 2-Tor put together chips and circuits. Finally you hold up a helmet. "Finished!" you say. "The hunt for the starsnipe is over."

"What good is that?" Longhaul says. "It doesn't even have eyeholes."

"You'll see," you say. "Let's get to the captain's cabin."

Go to page 79.

You leap for safety outside the Hive. Chaos is all around you. As you crash to the planet's surface, the Hive whispers in your brain. *"You ... have unleashed our stolen ... stellar energy.... Everything will be destroyed ... destroyed ... dest ..."* It fades away as the planet erupts around you.

"Scan the area, 2-Tor! Any trace of the Hive or the spiraloids?"

"Negative!" 2-Tor whistles. "They've been consumed. We'll join them shortly unless you think of something. Our power is very low."

"There's one chance!" you reply. "This is stellar energy raging around us. Tap into it with your energy collectors."

"Good idea, boss!" 2-Tor's lights flash green. "The energy will power our shields for as long as the starfire burns."

Your shields surround you. For a long time you watch the planet of the spiraloids burn to cinders around you. Finally you share the planet only with ashes. The Hive is gone for good.

"Access the *Nebula* for a lift," you tell 2-Tor. "We're going home."

*You have completed your mission.
Report to the* Nebula *on page 115
to find out how you rate as a Space Ace.*

104

You thoughtcast to the Hive, *"I've never seen a life form like you. Tell me about yourself."*

"You need know nothing more than your fate," the Hive beams back. You try to switch on your shields. But you can't move your hand. *"We have taken control of your body,"* the Hive says. *"You will not need it soon."*

You rise and float as the Hive takes you farther into itself. In the center there is a humanoid body many times larger than yours.

"We formed this body from the solidified light of a thousand stars," the Hive says. *"We created it to explore an unknown dimension we discovered. It is a place that might be too much for even the starbody. The starbody needs a mind to control it—your mind."*

If you go along with the Hive's plans, turn to page 108.

If you suggest a different plan, turn to page 100.

"That cored star is weird!" you tell 2-Tor. "Access the *Nebula*. We need a science officer out here."

Light flashes out of nowhere, and Dr. Leonus, a scientist from the *Nebula*, appears. He's a powerful-looking, razor-toothed humanoid, but a gentle scientist. "Let's see this star," he says.

Go to page 27.

106

"You should know why you have to die," Kobold says. "I stole a weapon that I like to call a sun destroyer. It blows up suns, creates them, steals their energy. It's wonderful! I'm going to use it to make the Network of Worlds pay me lots of money. I might destroy their suns anyway, just for fun. I like to destroy for fun. Of course, I have to destroy you first, or you'll give away my plans. Ready . . . aim . . ."

"*Wait!*" you shout. "My bio-support suit will detonate if I'm killed. Destroy me and the explosion will rip apart this ship!"

"He's bluffing," Kobold snarls. But the other aliens cringe and lower their weapons.

Kobold grabs a pulser and fires. Your bio-support suit explodes, taking the ship with you, as you promised. The commander and his sun destroyer are wiped out. "I've destroyed *myself,*" Kobold says with his dying breath. "That was *really* fun!" Then all of you float lifelessly in space.

ZAP!

It's obvious that the Saurans won't give up unless you scare them.

"Give the stellar-stealer just enough of a blast to dent the shell, 2-Tor," you thoughtcast. *"That should scare them."* A pulserbolt ripples from your suit across the metal skin of the stellar-stealer. The machine buckles. Light glows from beneath the metal. The Saurans scream and stop in their tracks.

"Don't destroy us!" the ancient Sauran hisses. "We surrender!"

"Why were you stealing stars?" you ask.

"We planned to smash the Network of Worlds with the energy. Then we would take over. We needed your warper so we could launch a sneak attack."

But the Saurans' schemes are finished. 2-Tor has already accessed the *Nebula.* Captain Polaris is sending a squad to take the Saurans to a prison asteroid. A science team will return the stolen energy to the stars.

You have completed your mission.
Report to the Nebula *on page 115*
to find out how you rate as a Space Ace.

108

"I'll mindmeld with your starbody on one condition," you thoughtcast to the Hive. "Stop stealing stars!" The Hive buzzes furiously, as if it were arguing with itself.

Finally it replies. "Agreed!" A spiraloid touches your forehead with its antennae. Your mind is yanked from your body and floats over the scene. Your body lies on the Hive floor, and spiraloids swarm over it. 2-Tor's sensors track the creature carrying your mind across the room.

The spiraloid burns up as it touches the starbody. For a long time you feel yourself falling into a bright light. You stand up and raise a hand in front of your eyes. The hand glows. You are in the starbody, filled with more power than you have ever felt.

There is a buzzing in your head, even though the Hive isn't casting thoughts at you. You realize that the starbody can read the Hive's mind. It doesn't know you can hear it. What you hear angers you. The Hive already plots to steal more stars. You know it won't live up to its part of the bargain. Should you keep your part?

If you carry out your part of the bargain, turn to page 32.

If you want to end the bargain, turn to page 19.

You snatch the beacon from Bront's hand. "I'm sorry," you say. "This is too important to leave up to a madman. Can we warp to the starsnipe and back, Tor?"

"Aye, aye, sir," 2-Tor whistles. "I mean . . . sure."

You disappear in a flash of light. Microseconds later you appear on the starsnipe's hide. It is rock. Up close the monster looks like an asteroid that stretches to infinity. You jam the beacon into a crack in the stone.

"Warp us back, 2-Tor."

"I can't, boss." His red lights blink. "A magnetic field here is messing up my circuits."

Bront's ships arrive. They crash into the starsnipe and burrow under its skin. The rocky skin begins to erupt. "So long, 2-Tor," you say. "It's been nice knowing you."

"You give up too easily, sports," Captain Bront says over your communicator. Gravity beams pull you and 2-Tor off the starsnipe. A moment later the monster falls apart, leaving space littered with stone. "We beat the beastie, we did!" Bront says. "My life is complete."

You have completed your mission.
Report to the Nebula *on page 115*
to find out how you rate as a Space Ace.

110

"That sunworm brainwave you picked up, 2-Tor. Is it any language we can understand?" you ask.

"I'm checking, boss. Did you know there are at least seven million languages currently spoken in the civilized galaxy? Three times as many were once used. . . . Hold it! It sounds like a language spoken by giants that live on the edge of the known universe. What have you got in mind?"

"Patch me into a mindlink if you can," you say. "Translate my thoughts into the language of the giants. I'm going to try to talk with the sunworm."

But even when the broadcast is sent, the monster doesn't answer. Instead, it devours the last bit of the star—and then it turns toward you.

If you want to keep trying to communicate, turn to page 52.

If you decide to defend yourself, turn to page 15.

"Nebula operatives don't squeal!" you tell the leader of the Vend. His eyes pop open wide with anger. "2-Tor! Access this starship's computers. We're taking over!"

"You can't do that," the leader says. He snickers. "That meganium toy is too small. It doesn't have the power."

"Don't be too sure. 2-Tor! Switch off the magnetic field that holds the star open in ten seconds. Stop only if this Vend clown surrenders."

"Boss . . ." 2-Tor's lights flash red. "There's something you should know . . ."

"Your robot wants to tell you that *I'm* linked into ship's computers," the Vend leader says. He pulls off his face. Computer chips and circuitry hum and glint all over its face.

"You're a robot," you gasp.

A crackling laugh erupts from the leader's head. "You'll never reveal my secret!"

A hatch opens. Like old garbage, you are dumped into the sun.

ZAP!

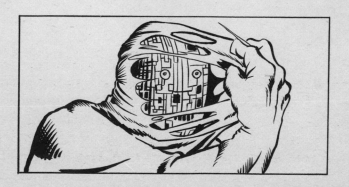

112

"Do you mean we should give that monster a cosmic bellyache?" the Attack Team leader gasps. "Even if your idea would work, we haven't got any free energy left!"

"The *Challenger* is burning up with energy," you reply. "We absorbed it from the stasis web."

"But there's only one way to get that energy into the sunworm—fly it in personally," the team leader says. "And that would kill you. Think of another plan."

If you think you can risk flying into the sunworm, turn to page 98.

If you'd rather think of another plan, turn to page 80.

114

"I know that creature is an intelligent being," you tell 2-Tor. "We can't take the chance of destroying it! We have to stop the Attack Team. We have to prove the sunworm thinks."

"There are signs of intelligence, boss," 2-Tor beeps. "Nothing I'd call conclusive."

"You know *Nebula* regulations, Tor. If there's even a question, we should preserve intelligent life." You zip the *Challenger* between the squad and the sunworm. A message crackles across your communicator.

"I don't care what your status on the *Nebula* is," the Attack Team leader says. "Get that shuttlecraft out of the way or we'll blow you to Ansales-C! You're protecting a threat to the Network of Worlds."

If you face off against the Attack Team,
turn to page 18.

If you try to prove the sunworm is intelligent,
turn to page 92.

WE MADE IT, BOSS!
REMEMBER THE
PAGE NUMBER YOU
CAME FROM, AND
CHECK THE SCORES
ON THE NEXT PAGE!

IF YOU WARPED IN FROM PAGE:
78, you get 8,775,504 points
107, you get 8,323,776 points

CONGRATULATIONS—
YOU'RE A SPACE ACE!

IF YOU WARPED IN FROM PAGE:
15, you get 431,532 points
52, you get 694,894 points
103, you get 769,960 points

IF CAPTAIN POLARIS
NEEDS A SECOND IN
COMMAND, HE'LL KNOW
WHERE TO LOOK.

IF YOU WARPED IN FROM PAGE:
26, you get 41,749 points
40, you get 58,430 points
41, you get 65,262 points
84, you get 36,400 points
86, you get 81,903 points
95, you get 94,600 points

NOT BAD! PUT IN SOME
TRAINING TIME ON THE
NEBULA COMPUTER.

IF YOU WARPED IN FROM PAGE:
82, you get 4,243 points
83, you get 9,987 points
91, you get 1,929 points
93, you get 5,809 points

YOU'RE ASSIGNED TO
ASTEROID PATROL UNTIL
FURTHER NOTICE.

IF YOU WARPED IN FROM PAGE:
48, you get 598 points
80, you get 847 points
81, you get 953 points

GO BACK TO THE SPACE
ACADEMY!

TO TRY ANOTHER ADVENTURE IN *EXPLODING SUNS*, GO TO PAGE 3.

OR

TO TAKE ON A COMPLETELY NEW CHALLENGE, GO TO *STAR CHALLENGE #5*: THE GALACTIC RAIDERS

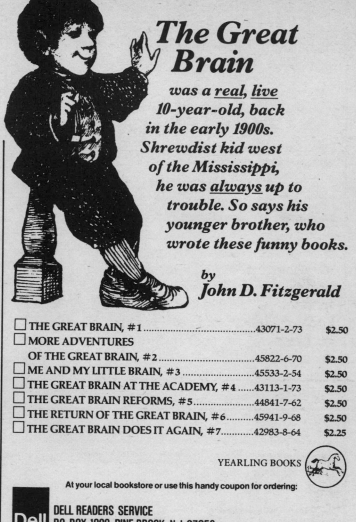